A meeting of minds. . . .

The Indian who stood there, filling the doorway, was the tallest man Samuel had ever seen. The two heron feathers that rose from the cap on his head brushed the roof of the Meetinghouse. Samuel could see that the Indian was at least a head taller than his own father, who was not a small man. Yet that big man had slipped in through the door of the cabin as quietly as a breath of wind crossing the meadow. The big Indian held a bow and arrow in his hand. He stood there calmly, looking around the Meeting, peering intently into one face after another.

Someone moved behind the tall man. It was an Indian boy. He too was tall, and held himself very straight. And while that tall man looked into the face of Samuel's father, the slender young Indian did something very strange. He lifted up a stone that he held in his right hand, shut one eye, and then squinted through the hole in the stone as if it were a spyglass. He surveyed the room and then looked through the hole directly at Samuel.

The Arrow Over the Door

Joseph Bruchac
Illustrated by James Watling

PUFFIN BOOKS

PUFFIN BOOKS
Published by the Penguin Group
Penguin Putnam Books for Young Readers,
345 Hudson Street, New York, New York 10014, U.S.A.
Penguin Books Ltd, 80 Strand, London WC2R ORL, England
Penguin Books Australia Ltd, Ringwood, Victoria, Australia
Penguin Books Canada Ltd, 10 Alcorn Avenue, Toronto, Ontario, Canada M4V 3B2
Penguin Books (N.Z.) Ltd, 182-190 Wairau Road, Auckland 10, New Zealand

Penguin Books Ltd, Registered Offices: Harmondsworth, Middlesex, England

First published in the United States of America by Dial Books for Young Readers,
a member of Penguin Putnam Inc., 1998
Published by Puffin Books,
a division of Penguin Putnam Books for Young Readers, 2002

1 3 5 7 9 10 8 6 4 2

THE LIBRARY OF CONGRESS HAS CATALOGED THE DIAL EDITION AS FOLLOWS:
Bruchac, Joseph, date.
The arrow over the door / Joseph Bruchac;
pictures by James Watling.—1st ed.
p. cm.
Summary: In the year 1777 a group of Quakers and a party
of Indians have a memorable meeting.
ISBN 0-8037-2078-5 (trade)
1. Indians of North America—New York (State)—Juvenile fiction.
[1. Indians of North America—New York (State)—Fiction.
2. Quakers—Fiction. 3. United States—History—18th century—Fiction.]
I. Watling, James, ill. II Title.
PZ7.B82816Ar 1998
[Fic]—DC20 96-36701 CIP AC

Puffin Books ISBN 0-14-130571-1

Printed in the United States of America

For all those who believe in peace

J.B.

1 COWARDS

Samuel

"There they go," a voice said. "There are the cowards."

Samuel Russell clenched his fists so tightly that his knuckles turned white, but he did not look around. He continued walking down the unpaved street with Father and Mother and Jonathan. The August sun was hot. Beads of sweat formed on Samuel's brow and upper lip, but he did not reach his hand up to wipe them away.

He knew that voice. It belonged to Nathaniel Moon. Only three years ago, when they were both boys, Nathaniel had played with him whenever his family came to this settlement to buy their supplies. They had made boats together out of pieces of wood from the mill and floated them down the swift-running Fish Creek at the edge of the town, watching them rush into the wide Hudson River. Now, though, it was different. Nathaniel was no longer his friend.

Nathaniel was going to be a drummer for Schuyler's regiment, taking the place of a boy who was shot in the retreat from Fort Edward. Nathaniel would go to fight against the British. He would march with the men and play his drum. He'd come home a hero.

But Samuel was not Nathaniel Moon. He'd never go to war. "Cowards," that was what many people called him and his father and all his people.

"Fighting is not our way," Father said, resting one hand on Samuel's muscular arm. "Love thine enemies. Thou must understand this."

Samuel said nothing, even though he clenched his teeth so tightly that his temples throbbed. But Jonathan, his brother, seemed to understand.

"To be a Friend is to be a friend to peace," Jonathan said. His tone was so much like that of Father that Samuel sometimes felt as if he were the little brother and Jonathan, though six years younger, the older one.

It was Jonathan who always remembered the stories Mother told of those Friends who had died for their beliefs. There had been a time when Friends had had to hide from those who would jail or kill them. Once, in England, when several Quaker parents were all taken away to jail, their children had faith so great that they continued to hold Meetings on their own. Jonathan would have been one of those children, Samuel thought.

He tried to recall those stories. It was no use. He could still hear Nathaniel's voice. It hurt so much to be called a coward, to have people look at you that way.

It had never been easy for his people to be accepted, but it had gotten worse since the war had begun. The Quakers made up only a few of the families settled on the east side of the Hudson at Saratoga in New York. Most of the settlers were Dutch, English, or German. Before the war began, there had been those who disliked the Friends, but there were at least as many who had treated them well enough. Perhaps they would not accept the hand of friendship held out to them— the shaking of hands was a Quaker custom that few wished to copy, for it implied equality on both sides. But there had once been many who would smile at them or engage in conversation. It was not that way any longer.

Things were so confused now, in the summer of 1777. Samuel knew there were some families besides the Friends who were neutral. Yet at times it seemed as if everyone was at war with everyone else. Some neighbors were Loyalists and said they would fight to defend King George. The Patriots said that they would fight for freedom from the king. Only a few seasons ago those people had been friends. Now they were ready to kill each other, even their blood relatives. They called each other Tories, supporters of the king, and Rebels, those who wanted the American colonies to be free from English rule. Even the Indians were divided: Some tribes fought for the king and some for the Americans, while some Indian villages or whole nations might have people fighting on both sides. And both sides suspected that the Quakers were giving comfort to the enemy, when Friends wished only to stay on the path of peace.

Samuel tried to find the Inner Light inside himself that would give him peace. He felt only confusion, like the confusion all around them in the settlement today.

A battle had taken place in Bennington just a week ago. Bennington was no more than a day's journey to the southeast. Since then many people had begun to leave Saratoga. Those people had already been fearful of what would happen if the British and their fierce Indian allies came. Now, since Bennington, everyone knew that the British general, Burgoyne, would come with his army. Battles would likely be fought not far from here. It was time to flee. Already most people to the north had left. Many of those who were secretly Loyalists stayed, though. They sat in their homes hoping for the sound of war. Half the mills, houses, and shops scattered through the settlement were deserted.

The shop of Tom Watt, the baker, was empty. Tom himself was boarding a window shut. Tom had always been friendly to the Russell family, tipping his hat to Father and Mother, his broad moon face beaming as he smiled at Samuel and Jonathan. But today he did not turn to look at them. A party of Loyalist raiders—cow boys as people now called them—had driven off Tom's best horse, his two cows, and all his pigs the day after Schuyler's retreat. Now Tom had no interest in the peace-loving Friends.

Tom Watt's family was packed and waiting. All their belongings were tied on to a cart that Tom had made himself, its wheels two big end pieces of log he had sawed off, with holes in the middle to fit on to the axletree. Tom clucked to their horse.

For a moment the cart would not move. Then finally it did, thumping and bumping as it went. The green wood wheels screeched like the whining puppy held by Tom's little daughter. She was sitting beside her mother as Tom walked next to the rough cart, which could not have held them all. Samuel watched as the Watt family rolled out of town. Perhaps they would never come back. Tom had always had a great fear of the Indians. He did not want to end up scalped.

A little shiver went down Samuel's back at the thought. A woman had been tomahawked and a family massacred by Indians that July in Fort Edward, only fifteen miles to the north. Father said that Indians were like all other people. But other people were not as understanding about Indians as Friends were. It did not matter if some of the Indians spoke English as well as any white person or prayed to the same Christian God, or even dressed in the same clothes as did their white neighbors. All Indians were dangerous savages to those people whose minds were closed against them.

Father patted him on the shoulder. "I am going to the blacksmith's shop. Stay with thy mother and thy brother."

Samuel nodded, feeling the return of a little pride. At fourteen he was almost a grown man, his chest nearly as broad as Father's, old enough to watch over Mother and Jonathan.

Father crossed over to the blacksmith's shop. Following close behind Mother and Jonathan, Samuel went into the general store. While Mother walked to the back of the store, Samuel and Jonathan drifted toward the group of men talking together at the front.

"Bennington," Brewster the storekeeper was saying, "horrible it was. British and Tories and Germans and Indians painted like so many devils."

"Think of how that poor Tory girl was killed by Burgoyne's own Indians! That Jane McCrea. Murdered by those fiends," said Restcombe Green. "And what will happen when such savages come here?"

"It has happened before," said old Wait Folliot. The clay pipe that seemed to be part of his hand made a circle of smoke as he lifted it up. "Remember when the French Indians burned Fort Saratoga in forty-five? Thirty killed and scalped, sixty poor souls taken to Canada to be tortured and killed or, worse yet, made into Indians or Papists? And I have heard it said that it is those same Canadian Indians who have come down to join with Burgoyne now."

"It is not the Canadians, but the fearsome Mohawk that do trouble me," Restcombe Green

broke in. "They cleave to the British out of love and loyalty to the spirit of Sir William Johnson. Three years dead he might be, but his nephew Guy is the Crown's Indian Commissioner in his place and more dangerous than was his uncle. And by his side is that Mohawk serpent, Joseph Brant. He might dress in fine clothes like an English gentleman, but he is a black-hearted demon who would see us all scalped."

"Mark you this," said Brewster, raising his voice, "the Tories such as Guy Johnson and his kind are as bad as any Indians, if not worse. Those Tory raiders went harrying on horseback all along the river, driving off people's livestock to feed their British masters. Where Johnson and Brant the Mohawk go, blood and fire will follow!"

Brewster's words brought Mother rushing from the back of the store, thoughts of shopping forgotten. The men stopped talking. They stared as she spread her arms—like a mother hen raising her wings—to shoo her two sons out of the store. Soon they were out the door, back in the burning heat of the sun.

"There is shade under the chestnuts. We shall wait there in *peace* for thy father," Mother said.

But as they walked toward the wide-branched

trees, there was little peace in Samuel's mind. Head down, he trailed a few paces behind his mother and his brother. Jonathan kept looking back at him anxiously. He had always been able to tell when Samuel was upset.

"We are Friends," Samuel whispered to himself. "Yet if any Loyalists or Indians should try to harm us, I will fight for my family!"

2 WARRIORS

Stands Straight

The tall boy who sat cross-legged in front of the Catholic church was dressed in much the same way as the French people in the nearby town of Trois-Rivières. Though his trousers and his shirt were the kind that could be seen from Montréal to the Gaspé Peninsula, his long black hair, the brown color of his skin, and the Algonquin features of his handsome face revealed the fact that he was an Indian. So did his moccasins and the leather pouch decorated with the beaded shape of a rabbit, which hung at his waist. One of the boy's slender hands rested lightly on that pouch.

As the boy sat there, his eyes focused on the river, the St. François, the French priest came past on his way to the sacristy.

"*Bonjour*, Piel," said the priest.

"*Bonjour, Pater* Louis," the boy answered, his gaze not shifting from the rippling St. François. His French was good. Aside from having a certain lilt, it was the same French spoken by the Platzmoniak, as his Abenaki people called the Frenchmen. Not everyone in Odanak could speak French as well as he did, but not everyone had been an altar boy.

Father Louis continued on into the church. He had lived long enough among the Indians to know that it was impolite to disturb someone when there was a silence upon him.

"Piel," the boy repeated. He stood in one easy motion and walked to the high bank above the river. Down there, he thought, is where my grandmother and my other relatives hid when the Bostoniak came to kill us all. He squatted down and began to speak in Abenaki.

"*Sibo,*" he said. "River, do you recognize the name Piel? *Nda!* No, you do not." He reached into his pouch and pulled out the stone that was his most prized possession. A perfectly round hole was in the center. His uncle had called it an eye stone.

"*Sassaskawinno,*" his uncle Sees-the-Wind had said to him, "Stands Straight. You can use this eye stone to see into the heart of things."

Stands Straight held the stone up and looked through it. He looked back at the village of Odanak and the new church that was not yet completely built. He looked at the neat log cabins and wood-frame wigwams in which most of his people had lived for two generations now—houses with doors and windows. These days almost all their houses were like these, no longer the old longhouses and circular homes covered with birch bark. Most of those old-style wigwams had been burned down by the Bostoniak—the Americans—when they came like a storm wind out of the night.

Then he turned and looked again at the river through his eye stone. The village might change, but the river did not. Even before his people had followed the bidding of the priests and come to settle close to the church in this little mission village, they had made their homes along the river. They knew its voices and its many moods. They knew how to ride through the currents of its rapids, there where the little underwater people lived. If an enemy tried to go through those rapids, the little underwater people would grab his canoe and tip it over. But if a friend came, the little underwater people would show him the way through.

"*Kwai, kwai, nidoba,*" said a voice from close behind him. Hello, hello, my friend.

"Hello, my older cousin," Stands Straight answered without turning around. "I heard you coming for the last fifty paces. You walk like a wounded moose."

"Ah," Wolf Marked said, dropping down onto a nearby log, "that is good. I have been practicing how to walk like a white man. Since we are to go south into the country of the Bostoniak, I thought I should learn their ways."

Stands Straight placed the eye stone back into its pouch and turned to look at his cousin. Wolf Marked was shorter and broader than he, but his face showed the age and experience that Stands Straight had yet to gain. There was a crooked scar across his older cousin's temple where he had been grazed by a Maguak arrow and the look in his eye was that of a man who has been in battle. On his right cheek was the birthmark that had given him his name, a brown shape that looked like a sitting wolf with its head raised to the sky.

Wolf Marked looked up at the bright late-summer sun and then gestured with his chin upriver. "The blueberries will be ripe. Remember how many we picked two summers ago?"

Stands Straight nodded. Since the French armies

had lost Canada to the Songlismoniak—the English—and King George, there had been a few years of relative peace for his people. There had been time for such things as berry picking and hunting, without the fear of being caught between their armies. Now, though, with the Bostoniak rebelling against King George, war had come again and was spreading. Perhaps it would even come up here.

"Why has King George asked us to join him?" Stands Straight said.

Wolf Marked pulled out his knife and began to jab it into the log. "It is because the Huron and Ottawa and Wyandot who were fighting for him have gone home. They became disgusted with King George. I hear it is because a Bostoniak woman was killed. Some Ottawas were taking her to safety and the Bostoniak shot at them. The Bostoniak bullets killed her. But the Indians were blamed for her death. The Songlismoniak scolded the Ottawa and Wyandot and Huron as if they were small stupid children. Also the Songlismoniak did not give them the clothing and food and other goods that had been promised to them. So the Ottawa and Wyandot and Huron decided it would be better for them to go home and take care of their cornfields. And because King George understands that we are great warriors, he has come to us—even though we are far fewer—to take their places."

"And so King George asks us to take their place, knowing we were not his friends? Knowing that our fathers and grandfathers fought by the side of the French?"

"King George does not care if we are friends. He just asks us to fight and die for him. The Songlismoniak and Bostoniak do not know the meaning of friend," Wolf Marked continued, sticking the point of his knife deeper into the log. "You accept their ways and they still come to your village in the night and kill all of your people. Not just the warriors, but the children and the old ones as well."

Stands Straight nodded. Wolf Marked was old enough to remember what had been done to their village by the Bostoniak. It had happened four years before Stands Straight was born. Rogers and his Rangers had attacked when no one was there but old people and women and children. Many had died in that coward's raid.

Wolf Marked wrenched his knife out of the log and then drove it in again, deeper than before. "They burned our church, they even killed our French priests! *Sacré bleu!*"

Wolf Marked spoke the French language nearly as well as his young cousin. After having the French and their priests among them for more than a century, most of the Abenaki people had some familiarity with the language. The French and the Abenaki had grown close in more ways than one. Some of the Frenchmen, like their friend Richard, seemed more Abenaki than white.

Stands Straight smiled when he thought of Richard, who was the age of Wolf Marked and often tagged along behind him. Richard tried to make himself look even more Indian than his Abenaki friends. While they wore shirts of French cloth and ornaments made of brass and silver, Richard would wear only clothing made of animal skins decorated with porcupine quills.

"You are smiling, Cousin?" Wolf Marked asked.

"I am thinking of Richard," said Stands Straight.

Wolf Marked laughed. "*Oui, oui! Mon Platzmoni sauvage.* Today I found him trying to pluck the hairs from his face as we do. I told him that a bear would have better luck in making its face smooth that way. A bear has fewer hairs on its face than does Richard! Ah, but I like the man. I am glad that he will be going with us. He is no Bostoni." Wolf Marked frowned and then said the only words he knew in English. "A curse on the Bostonians!"

"I understand now why King George wants us to fight for him," Stands Straight said. "But why are we going to answer his call? Is it because of what the Bostoniak have done to us?"

"Ask our uncle," said Wolf Marked. "He is leading us."

"I shall do so."

When Stands Straight reached the house of his uncle, the place where he had lived since his father died, he found Sees-the-Wind standing in front of his door, waiting for him. It was always that way with Sees-the-Wind. He seemed to know what things would happen before they happened. No one ever went to the wigwam of Sees-the-Wind at any time of the day or night without finding the tall, gray-haired man waiting for him, the hint of a smile on his face.

"Your aunt has made soup and baked bread," Sees-the-Wind said.

After they had eaten and his uncle had taken out his pipe and lit it, Stands Straight asked his question about why they would go to help the British with their fighting.

"It is better for some of us to go and see what is happening," Sees-the-Wind said.

Although his uncle said nothing more, Stands Straight understood. "Let the whites all kill each other." That was what some of the people in Odanak had suggested. Then the land would be empty of them, and the Abenaki people could live as they did long ago.

But Stands Straight knew that it was not a good thing for the whites to fight each other. There were too many of them now to wipe each other out. Once again his people were being drawn in. It would probably be as it had been before, when the French and English fought their many wars. Whenever fighting took place between the white people, it was always the Indians who got the worst of it. But if some went and saw, at least they would learn what the worst of it might be.

3 RIPPLES

▼

Samuel

Samuel rested his hands carefully on the rough stones so that he could lean out over the water. It might be dangerous now to come alone to the brook, but this had always been his favorite place. The sun had just risen and he knew no one would be at the brook this early. And though it was Fifth Day, their Meeting would not take place until the sun was higher in the sky. He could be back home and ready before Father or Mother even noticed he was missing.

Everyone else in their house—Father, Mother, even Jonathan—was thinking about the Meeting. A special guest would be there, a Friend named Robert Nisbet. Though he lived at East Hoosuck, more than thirty miles distant, he had felt a concern to walk all that way to sit with them at their Meeting.

Samuel, though, did not share their thoughts. He had needed to find solitude, so he had come to the brook.

It was quiet in the eddy here below a waterfall. Samuel moved very slowly above the little pool. That way he would not disturb the fish that sometimes came here, great trout so large they could break any line. He never thought of catching them. He just watched them and imagined what their lives were like, there in the flow of the brook. They never had to pick up stones or fetch water or cut wood. All they had to do was swim and eat and avoid being caught. They had so few troubles.

But when he looked down, the pool was empty. All he saw was his own reflection. There, five feet below him, was the wavery image of a broad-shouldered farm boy dressed in a homespun shirt. That boy was almost of a man's height, yet his smooth cheeks were not yet those of a man. His serious face, with its wide blue eyes and bump of a nose, was shaded by a thatch of yellow-brown hair as thick as a mound of late-summer hay.

Samuel frowned, and the image on the surface of the water frowned back at him. He would much rather have seen a trout. Or the reflection of someone whose life was more exciting than his, someone like Nathaniel Moon. He wondered what had happened to Nathaniel in the weeks that had passed since he saw him last. Had he marched bravely before the men, beating his drum with the sounds of guns and cannons all around him? Samuel had seen Nathaniel's mother last week and had thought to speak to her. He had come close, but when he saw how pained and worried her face was, he had said nothing.

It was now September. Though the great battles that had long been expected had not yet happened, everyone knew that they would come soon enough. All the settlers had been warned to leave the area. The countryside was filled with parties of men moving about. Armies were marching to the west and the south. There were rumors of scouts and spies, Indians and Loyalist cow boys. Everyone kept a close watch on their livestock, and no animals were left out in the fields at night. No one knew what would happen next.

Samuel picked up a large pebble and dropped it into the water. His reflection broke into a cascade of rippling light and then formed again. He stared at it, wondering how another face might look, reflected back from that pool. The face of a soldier or a drummer boy, the face of a Patriot or a Loyalist—

even the face of an Indian! Samuel sat back on his heels and looked around. For a moment he had felt as if someone were watching him. But there was no one to be seen.

Samuel lifted up his hands and held the palms in front of his face. They were broad and strong, thickly calloused from working in the fields. These hands could hold a gun, he thought. Perhaps not in a battle of armies, but at home, to protect us from the Indians.

Almost everyone else had guns in their houses. Some farmsteads were now like small fortresses, their thick wooden doors banded with metal and double-barred.

But Father and the others in the Saratoga Meeting had no locks on their door. And no Friend would have a gun, a weapon that might injure other human beings. Even when they went to work in their fields, many of the other people carried guns with them now. But no weapons were ever carried to the fields of Friends.

Samuel shook his head as he thought of the fields.

"Lower Field," he said, "I love thee not, for thou art filled with rocks which I must grub out and pile into walls."

At least on this Meeting day he would escape

the toil of gathering stones to clear the lower field. He dropped another pebble into the water. The ripples made him think of plowed furrows. A long stick had washed close to the bank. He leaned over and pulled it out. It was a maple branch, washed for so long by the waters that it was almost as smooth as a hoe.

Samuel stood and held the branch in his hands. It was thicker than a hoe and felt good in his hands. He hoisted it to his shoulder. Would a musket feel like this? He let it drop and then held it in one hand, pretending for a moment that it was a spear he might throw.

Then he let one end drop to the ground. This, he thought, is the only way I will ever get to use it—as a walking stick. He tossed it aside and turned to walk away. But as he did, he slipped on the wet moss at the edge of the brook. His foot twisted painfully as he fell on the damp ground.

When Samuel stood up, it hurt to put his weight on his ankle. Balancing with difficulty, he bent over and picked up the stick again. Though it would never serve him as a weapon, he thought, it could be of some use as a cane. Leaning on it, he limped back toward the farm.

More than a hundred feet of new fence wall along the edge of that same lower field marked Samuel's labors for the past three months. He stopped to look at the fence with a mixture of pride and resentment. As many stones as he and Father and Jonathan had picked up, there were always more still.

Samuel lifted up his head and listened. He thought he had heard a noise. Was it something hitting the ground there in the woods behind him? Perhaps the sound of a branch knocked free by a hawk as it took flight? He looked up and around, but his keen eyes saw no sign of a hawk. Maybe it was the sound of a musket being fired very far away. Such sounds were common now, and they echoed a great distance over the hills. But usually guns were heard just before dusk, when parties of men were moving back to their camps for the night. Then nervous soldiers would fire at things they saw, more often shadows than real enemies.

Samuel shook his head. Perhaps he had imagined the sound. He looked back toward the direction of the brook. It was screened from his view by the elm trees, but he could feel its presence. Then he looked up toward the house and the small family grave-yard on the hill above it. The morning sun was just touching the hill. No gravestones stood on the burial place. It was not the custom of the Friends to mark the graves of those who died. But Samuel knew their names.

"Israel, Rebecca, Patience, Hannah, Benjamin," Samuel said, repeating their names as he had so many times before. He felt as if he knew them all well, even though his older brothers and sisters had died before he was born.

None of them had lived as long as his younger brother Jonathan. Whooping cough and fevers had taken them all. And since Jonathan's difficult birth, it seemed that Mother could have no more children. It was hard enough to run a farm like theirs with a large family to do all the work. With only the four of them it was almost impossible. True, the Friends at Meeting could always be counted upon to help at the times of planting and harvest. All of them had come to help the Russells with the raising of the small barn. But the help of neighbors was not day-to-day. Day-to-day was the family.

Samuel looked back over his shoulder, tempted to look down just once more at the brook. He took a step toward the elm trees. Then he stopped. Early as it was, he would soon be missed. He turned and, again leaning on his stick, hobbled on toward the house without looking back.

4 ▼ ELDER BROTHER'S PATH

Stands Straight

The light of Elder Brother Sun shone from the morning edge of the sky. Stands Straight looked up into the sky from the wooded edge of the brook, below the falls. His hands were raised toward the warmth of the new day. Out of the corner of his eye he could see his uncle, who stood a hundred yards behind him by the edge of a thickly wooded valley.

Stands Straight knew that Sees-the-Wind was watching him. He could tell that his uncle was pleased that he was not forgetting to pray to the Creator and give thanks to Elder Brother Sun. After all, it was known that Elder Brother Sun liked the sight of war. And it was the path of war, Elder Brother's Path, that they were now walking.

But, as he stood giving thanks, the tall Abenaki

boy remained watchful. It had been three weeks since their party of six had set out from their little village. Now there were armies all around them and they were close to one of the towns of the Bostoniak. The white colonists who were rebelling against their king—"those cursed Bostonians," as Wolf Marked continued to call them—were known to be a dangerous and unpredictable people.

But the Songlismoniak, the so-called allies of the Abenaki, were nearly as bad. Twice, Stands Straight and the others had almost been shot by the British. The first time was just as they entered the British camp. They had come out of the evening so silently that they startled a soldier who was on sentry duty. He had lifted his musket to fire at them. Sees-the-Wind was too quick for the sentry, though. He had used his own musket like a club, knocking the other gun from the startled man's hands as it discharged harmlessly into the air. Then, even though the British soldier tried to protest, he had picked up the man's gun and taken it to an officer who could speak some French.

"*Pardon, mon ami.* This man would do better with a shovel in his hands," Sees-the-Wind had told the officer as he handed him the gun. "I am not happy because he tried to shoot me. *You* should not be happy because he missed."

The second time they had almost been shot was because of a pig. It nearly made Stands Straight laugh to think about it. The man they called Hungry Frenchman, who had traveled with them from Odanak to fight for the English, had found the pig rooting around near the edge of a field. He had tied a rope about its neck and brought it back. Making signals that the pig would be their meal, the Frenchman, who spoke almost no Abenaki, had tied the pig to a bush and gathered a handful of dry sticks.

"Bon cochon, bon cochon," Hungry Frenchman had kept saying. Good pig, good pig. His mouth was clearly watering at the thought of eating pig meat. It was so funny to watch, that all of them had been laughing, even Richard. Hungry Frenchman was a skinny, lantern-jawed man with a heavy beard. No matter how much he ate, he never got fat and he was always hungry. Before Sees-the-Wind could stop him, Hungry Frenchman had taken out his flint and steel and started a fire.

It was not a good place to start a fire. The grass was thick and dry and it began to burn. A great pillar of smoke rose up. Hungry Frenchman tried to put out the fire, but it was too late. As he batted at the grass with his hands, soldiers who had seen

the smoke arrived from both sides of the field. The soldiers in one group were Hessians, Germans hired to fight for King George. The men in the other group were Bostoniak.

Stands Straight and the others had scrambled away as fast as they could, while shots were fired at them from both sides! No one had been hurt, not even the pig, which slipped free of its rope and escaped into a hedgerow. But they had been in real danger. It was that second episode which had made his uncle decide that their small party would do better on its own, rather than staying close to the unpredictable white soldiers of King George.

That was yesterday. When a short British officer gave them their assignment, later the same day, Sees-the-Wind had squatted down to listen. They would be with Peter's Corps, one of the Loyalist regiments fighting by the side of the British. As soon as the officer finished talking, Sees-the-Wind stood up. He was almost twice as tall as the officer.

"We scout," Sees-the-Wind told the Peter's Corps officer. And scout they did, staying as far away from both armies as possible. One of the things they had scouted was this quiet camping place near the brook, which reminded them of their own river at Odanak.

I must finish my prayer, Stands Straight thought.

"Ktsi Nwaskw," he said, in a voice so soft that only the wind could hear it, "Great Mystery, you have kept us from harm. For that I give you thanks. All I ask is that you help us see the right road to follow. *Ktsi wliwini,* great thanks." Then he lowered his arms.

The sound of a crow came from the wooded valley behind him. It was one of their signals. Stands Straight moved away from the edge of the brook. As smoothly as a mink slipping among the rocks, he vanished from sight.

A few moments later he rose silently out of the brush to stand by the side of Sees-the-Wind. Stands Straight saw the hint of a smile on the face of his tall uncle. Sees-the-Wind was pleased.

I heard his warning call and did as I was supposed to do. He knows that his nephew's ears are good, Stands Straight thought. Though I am only fourteen winters old, he sees that I am learning the lessons of survival well.

Sees-the-Wind nodded at Stands Straight and then looked up at Elder Brother Sun.

"I have asked our Elder Brother if it is really war that he wants for us," he said. "But so far the Sun has not answered."

They heard the soft scrape of a moccasin on stone behind them.

"Did you get a good one?" Stands Straight asked, without turning around.

Wolf Marked stepped in front of his cousin and their uncle, holding up his spear. He was smiling. The trout on the spear was a big one, so long that its tail touched the ground as the wide young man with the brown wolf on his cheek held out the spear.

"I found them in the pool below the cliffs," Wolf Marked said. "This fish said it wished to join our war party. It was the smallest one, but I took pity on it."

"You did well," Sees-the-Wind said. "No fire, though. We are too close to the farms of the white people. Remember what happened to our Hungry Frenchman yesterday?"

Wolf Marked nodded. "A curse on the Bostonians. This fish is not as big as Hungry Frenchman's pig. But it will taste good raw."

Sees-the-Wind made a circling motion with one hand and cupped the other toward his mouth. Then he touched his hand lightly on the shoulders of each of his nephews in turn, before swinging that hand back toward the sunset direction where they had left Richard and Hungry Frenchman at the cave in the hills. A small spring bubbled from the rocks there.

Stands Straight and Wolf Marked understood. Taking the big trout, they went to gather the others. They would lead them back to that cave where they would eat and rest.

After the meal Stands Straight went outside the cave to wait. His uncle, along with Richard and Hungry Frenchman, was sitting just inside the mouth of the cave. Wolf Marked stood watch at the end of the clearing, so that no one could come upon them unawares. Watches-the-Hawk was not back. He had gone to scout farther upstream and had not yet returned. He had the best eyes of all of the men in their party. He was usually the one who took the lead, scouting ahead.

Stands Straight held the eye stone up and looked through it.

"I will see Watches-the-Hawk," he said. "He will come down that deer path toward us."

The eye stone had been given to Stands Straight by the deep spring which never dried up in the hottest summer or froze in the coldest winter. The stone was small enough to cup in the palm of his hand. It was smooth and rounded like the egg of a wood duck. Its color was the kind of blue he had seen only in the sky. You could see the spirit that trembled in everything when you looked through the hole in the center.

Wherever he went, he carried the eye stone with him in the deerskin pouch that hung at his waist. He remembered the morning six winters ago when the stone was given to him.

Sees-the-Wind had wakened him at first light. It was the job of an uncle to show his nephew the right way to live.

"Today," Sees-the-Wind had said, "you must find something that will be a helper to you. You have lived through eight winters. So it is time for you to do this."

It was a very cold morning. There was mist over the waters of the pool where the deep spring bubbled up. There was ice around the edge of the spring, but the center of the pool was clear.

Sees-the-Wind had looked at him and then made two motions with his hands—a sweeping gesture toward the water and then a downward thrust with the fingers of his hands pressed together.

Stands Straight was used to the cold. Each morning in the little village everyone went out to bathe at first light in the nearby stream. But he knew this would not be easy.

Sharp edges of ice had cracked against his legs as he waded in. Then, where it became deep, he dove down as his uncle had told him to do. But he did not reach the bottom. He floated back up, bent at the waist, and kicked. His eyes were open, but the water was so cold that everything seemed blurred. He found nothing with his out-reached hands. When he came to the surface again, it seemed as if his lungs were on fire. But he dove a third time. This time he almost reached the bottom, but again he had to struggle back up for breath.

When he came to the surface that third time, he saw the worry on the face of his uncle. But then Stands Straight remembered the story his uncle had told him when he was a small child, about how Earth was created. There was no dry land. Everything was covered with water. So the birds and animals dove down to bring up some dirt that could be used to make dry land. The first three failed, but the last animal, Muskrat, brought up a pawful of dirt.

With that story in his mind, he had tried a fourth time. He had gone deeper than before. His hand had touched something so smooth that it felt warm as he grasped it. He had risen back up to the surface, holding the blue stone.

That was how the eye stone had been given to Stands Straight six winters ago.

Now, as he looked through it, he saw Watches-the-Hawk coming along the path, just as he had hoped.

Stands Straight turned back toward the cave and whistled the call of the redbird. Everyone was on their feet and waiting by the time Watches-the-Hawk joined them.

"I have seen the enemy," he said. "I have been to their houses and looked in their windows. They are beginning to gather in a cabin two looks from here." Then he laughed. "None of them have any eyes. Though I watched them, none of them saw me."

Wolf Marked handed him a piece of the pink meat of the trout. Watches-the-Hawk sat on the log by the cave mouth and ate while the others waited.

"I almost took a captive," he said. "A boy about your height, Stands Straight. I came close enough for him to almost feel my breath. He was looking into the brook the same way you look into your stone. We could have brought him back to our village with us to take the place of your brother who . . ."

Watches-the-Hawk stopped talking. As good as his eyes were, he had a problem with his mouth. He had never learned when to talk and when not to talk of certain things. He did not apologize for the pain that he saw in Stands Straight's eyes, but he was sorry in his heart.

All of Stands Straight's immediate family had taken the long road that led from the top of the highest mountain along the road of stars into the sky land. His father, whose name was Good Thunder, became ill and died soon after the birth of Stands Straight's brother. Stands Straight did not remember much about his father, aside from his smile and the sound of his voice telling stories about Great Hare.

But only two winters had passed since Stands Straight's mother and his brother and four others, all women and children, had left their village. They had gone south, far down the river, to trade. They had not returned. The story was brought back to them by a Mahican man who was a friend. He had told how those six were murdered by a band of armed Bostoniak men, crazy with drink and ready to kill any Indian they could find.

Had such a thing happened not long before, the Abenaki would have sought out those murderers. They would have taken Bostoniak lives in return.

But the elders of the village had listened to the words of Father Louis. Although many of the young men protested, they had not sent out a revenge party. Instead the men who left the village went with only one mission. They went to bring back the bones of their dead to bury them in the graveyard at Odanak.

When they returned, Father Louis held a special Mass for those who had been killed. All through that Mass and the days that followed, Stands Straight had wondered many things. He had wondered if the pain he felt in his heart would ever leave him. He had wondered why he did not feel that same desire for revenge that his friends felt, even though it was not their mother or brother who had been murdered. He had looked through the eye stone at the church, at the river, at the people around him. He had not seen the answers. That was one of the reasons his uncle had brought him on this journey. Perhaps the answers would be seen here in the land of the Bostoniak.

Watches-the-Hawk was looking down at the knife sheathed at his belt. Stands Straight could see that the sheath had broken yet again, and his friend was trying to mend it. He could also see, even though his friend tried to hide it, that Watches-the-Hawk still felt sorry in his heart.

Stands Straight reached into his pouch and pulled out a piece of rawhide. Then he walked over to his side and held out his hand.

"*Nidoba*," he said, "my friend, you can mend it with this."

"*Wliwini*," asked Watches-the-Hawk as he took the rawhide.

Sees-the-Wind slapped his hands once. The sound was like a beaver's tail striking the water. Everyone turned to look at him. He rubbed his palms together, then squatted down. The others gathered around him.

"This is what we will do," he said. "The Bostoniak are gathering. Perhaps they are among those who wish to fight the Songlismoniak king. We will scout this meeting. If the Bostoniak try to fight us, we will know they are not loyal to their king, and we will attack them. The little officer of the king's army is sure to reward us for this action."

Sees-the-Wind looked at the faces of each of the young men in turn. He saw no questions in any of them, except in the face of Stands Straight. The boy was not looking at his uncle. Instead his eyes were turned down.

"My nephew," Sees-the-Wind said, "what question do you have?"

Stands Straight looked up from the eye stone that he held in the palm of his right hand.

"Uncle," he asked, "do we know what is in the hearts of these people?"

Sees-the-Wind nodded. It was the kind of question he would have asked when he was a young man.

"My nephew," Sees-the-Wind said, "we will soon find out."

5 FATHER'S STORY

Samuel

As they sat together at the end of their breakfast, Samuel looked around the table at his family. He was worried. If fighting should come, what would happen to them? Samuel knew that today was to be a special day. Not only would those of the recently formed Saratoga Meeting be there, but Robert Nisbet would be joining them. The visiting Friend was staying at the farm of Zebulon Hoxsie, who had built the new Meetinghouse near his hilltop home.

Samuel looked over at his younger brother. He could see the pleased expression on Jonathan's face. His brother was always happy when there were new people to meet. There would also be children of Jonathan's own age at Meeting. Because they were Friends, they would understand the peace that comes when the Spirit of God dwells within. They would not look strangely at Jonathan in the way that some of the children who were not Friends did. It had always been that way for them. Wherever Friends went, those who did not share their faith might not understand them.

However hard he tried, Samuel could not think about Meeting. His thoughts kept going back to the brook, to the ripples that spread across the water as he dropped in his stones. Those ripples spread so wide. And war would be the same way. It would spread across the land and everyone would be touched by it. What can I do to protect our family? he wondered.

"Father," Samuel said, breaking the silence that was so familiar to all of them. It startled him how loud his own voice sounded. He had not meant to speak with such force.

Father turned his head and looked at Samuel with serious eyes, which were as blue as those of his sons. He leaned forward on his elbow. It was what Father did when he was truly listening to someone.

"Yes, Samuel?" he asked.

"What shall we do when the war comes here?"

"We shall do what we always do. We shall treat

all with charity and trust in the Truth of God, which changeth not."

Father's voice was deep and gentle. His words were as plain as his clothing. When Samuel was worried, it usually helped him to hear his father speak. Father was as solid as the foundation of their home or the stone walls they built around the fields. But today those words did not calm the thoughts rippling through Samuel's head. He looked down toward his plate.

Mother reached out a hand and brushed the hair from his forehead. Samuel looked out of the corner of his eye at his mother and thought how beautiful she was in her simple dark dress.

Then Mother looked directly at Samuel.

"What is troubling thy heart, Samuel?"

Samuel felt confused. He looked at her and then at Father, who was still leaning over the table, his chin cupped in his hand.

"What . . . what about the Indians and the Loyalists?" Samuel stammered.

He paused and looked around the table. Jonathan had one eyebrow raised, but said nothing.

"They said in Brewster's store that when battle comes, the Indians will sweep through here with blood and fire. Will they not kill us all? Should we

not leave here and go someplace where we will be safe?"

"Samuel," Mother said, "thou must remember that we have always sought friendship with the Indians. Many of them know us and are friends to us in return. They are children of God also. Is not that so, Father?"

Father was still for a moment. Then he said, "Let me tell thee a story. It is a tale of the great founder of our Society, George Fox himself. As thou well knoweth, he came here to the colonies and traveled far and wide, seeking those whose hearts were open. Each place he went he found those who had a sense of the power of God, who received the truth and did abide by it."

Samuel clenched his fists under the table. The stories of George Fox were frequently told by his father, who loved to study the history of the Society of Friends and often shared that history with his two sons. Too often, Samuel thought. I have heard this story before. Should we not be on our way to Meeting? He knew some of the other Friends would already be seated there, and the Meetinghouse was over a mile away. But Jonathan leaned forward and listened intently to Father's words.

"In 1672," Father continued, "George Fox

came to Carolina. There was a small band of Friends there. With Indians as their guides, they traveled along the Chowan River to reach the governor's house at Edenton. Their journey had not been easy, for the river grew so shallow that their boat would not swim and they were fain to put off their shoes and stockings and wade some distance through the water.

"The governor and his wife received them lovingly. But a doctor at the house of the governor would needs dispute their faith. The doctor denied that the Light and Spirit of God was in everyone. 'It is not in the Indians,' said the doctor. 'All that is within them is darkness, and they have neither conscience nor faith.'

"George Fox listened to the doctor. Then he looked about the room and called to him one of the Indians who had guided them to the governor's house. 'When thou dost lie or do wrong,' he said to the Indian, 'be there not something in thee that reproveth thee for it?' Then the Indian answered. 'Yes,' said the Indian, 'there is such a thing in me that reproveth me and maketh me ashamed.' So it was that the doctor himself was shamed before the governor and all the people."

Samuel looked over at his mother in exasperation. Perhaps she would understand his fears.

"It is our way, Samuel," she said with a smile. "We shall walk in peace and trust that others will see the Light within themselves."

Samuel said nothing. As Mother began to clear the bowls away, he stood and limped to the corner where he had leaned the walking stick. He picked it up and held it in his hands. Its weight comforted him. In the Scriptures, he thought, Samson used the jawbone of an ass to slay the army of the Philistines. This stick could serve him like that jawbone.

As they walked out of the house, Samuel was the last to leave. Leaning on his stick, he pulled the door of their cabin closed, so that the latch caught and the wind would not blow it open. There was no lock on the door, no bar to hold it shut when they were within.

In the settlement, whenever someone left a house or a shop, he would always secure it. The shopkeeper would pull out a ring of keys and lock that door tightly so that no one could enter unbidden. Samuel remembered walking along the street one afternoon at the end of the day and hearing the heavy sound of a bolt thudding into place, the rattle of keys hung on the great brass ring that swung from storekeeper Brewster's leather belt.

"Father," Samuel said now, "why do we have no lock on our door?"

"We have no need to keep anyone out," Father said. "If someone weary from travel should come to our door when we are not home, they can come in and take their rest."

"And what if that person wishes to steal from us?" Samuel asked stubbornly.

Father smiled. "A locked door will not keep out a man who is determined to steal from thee. He will simply break that door and come in to take what he wishes to take. Then thy door is lost, and so is whatever has been stolen. But an open door may lead a man to open his heart."

Father started walking, then turned back.

"There is also this to remember, Son. A great lock on a door tells a thief of the fear that what is within will be stolen. But a door without a lock tells the man who wishes to enter that nothing will be kept from him. Now come, we do not want to be late to Meeting."

Samuel sighed and tightened his grip on the walking stick.

"I wish that we did have locks," he whispered to himself. Then he turned to join his family.

6 THE OPEN DOOR

Stands Straight

Through a break in the stone wall that hid him from sight, Stands Straight watched the people who entered the house. His uncle had given him this task, to scout the enemy. Stands Straight was determined to do it well.

He watched through the circle of his eye stone and counted them as they arrived. Twelve so far. He saw that it was as his uncle had said. There were not a great many of these people and it did not look as if any of them would be strong fighters. His uncle had said to wait until all the Bostoniak were inside. Then their party would approach the cabin from their hiding places in all directions.

Stands Straight closed his eyes to imagine what would happen if there was fighting. If they set fire to the house, some would come out and try to put out the flames. That would be the time to strike. If the people did not struggle too much, then they could take them captive. If the Bostoniak fought too hard, some of them would be badly hurt or killed.

When one made a raid, Sees-the-Wind had explained, one had to do it quickly, as quickly as a hawk striking a rabbit. The smoke from a burning cabin would draw others, but by then it would be too late.

Stands Straight was not afraid of fighting. But he found himself wondering once more about these people they were about to fight. He lifted up his eye stone again.

As always, through that stone he saw things more clearly. He saw how these whites walked. The way people walked told much about them. Some of the Bostoniak walked more confidently than others. But none of them walked like warriors. He saw how some of the men and women who came walked alone. He saw the way some of the people walked together as families. Those four just arriving were clearly a family.

The woman, surely the mother, walked with the quick steps of a doe, looking back to be sure her fawns were with her. The father walked as a bear does, a slow, rolling walk. The older of the brothers: There was anger in his walk, even though he was limping and leaning on a walking stick. His shoulders were hunched, his chin down. He moved like a wolf, smelling the ground, sniffing the air, alert. Looking at him through the eye stone, Stands Straight could see that he was one who would be a good friend and a dangerous enemy. This must be the boy who Watches-the-Hawk had thought of capturing. The one who Watches-the-Hawk had said could become his brother, to take the place of Breaks-the-Sticks, who was killed by the crazy white men.

Then there was the younger brother.

Stands Straight watched the smaller boy closely. He looked to be the age Stands Straight had been when he found the eye stone, the age of his own younger brother when he had died.

It was hard to think of his younger brother. Sometimes when Stands Straight closed his eyes, Breaks-the-Sticks was there before him, looking just as he had looked when he was alive. His little brother had been quick to laugh and even quicker to play. Nothing ever made him angry, and no one was ever angry at him. Even though he always played tricks on people, Breaks-the-Sticks had been loved by everyone. It was good to see his little brother that way, held in the eye of his memory. But sometimes when Stands Straight tried to remember his brother, he did not see him alive. He saw him covered with blood, shot many times, the laughter stolen from his face forever.

Looking through the eye stone at the young Bostoniak boy, Stands Straight could see that he was not one to laugh and play jokes. He was not like Breaks-the-Sticks had been. He was more serious. But Stands Straight could also see that this boy could make a good younger brother. He would be sure that this boy was not hurt when the raid began.

The last of them had gone into the cabin now. It was not a very well-built cabin. The ones they built in their village at Odanak were much better. This cabin had been so roughly made, you could see between the logs. Cold winds would cut through like knives. It was strange.

Perhaps this was only a place for them to have their councils, thought Stands Straight. They had not shut the door behind them when they went in. Instead the door had been left partly open, the way one of his own people might leave open the flap of a lodge, to show that visitors were welcome. That was strange too. Then Stands Straight realized there was yet another strange thing: what he had *not* seen. At this time when war and the possibility of battle swirled around them all like the northern storm winds, not one of those white people had been carrying a gun.

Stands Straight turned and made hand motions toward the forest: All are inside. No guns.

Sees-the-Wind nodded and signaled back to his nephew, his hand held out and his palm toward the ground. *Stay there. Do not move.* He turned and did the same to the other men, who were well-hidden farther back among the trees. Stay. Do not move.

As Stands Straight watched through his eye stone, his uncle lifted up his head and looked at the cabin. He moved forward and climbed over the wall. Then Sees-the-Wind stood up in plain sight of the cabin. Stands Straight did not know how his uncle could stand there so calmly. His own heart was pounding so hard that he felt as if a partridge were lodged in his chest and beating its wings to escape.

Stands Straight turned slightly so that he could look through the eye stone at the small wooden lodge into which the white people had gone. Then he saw what his uncle saw. There, where the logs were unchinked to a space the width of three fingers, someone was looking out, straight at Sees-the-Wind. Stands Straight could see the wide eyes

and the pale cheeks of the one who looked out. And he knew who it was. It was the boy that Watches-the-Hawk had wanted to capture.

Suddenly the pounding in Stands Straight's heart stopped. He felt calm and he also felt afraid. His fear was no longer for himself but for the boy who looked out from that crack between two worlds, their world of forests and rivers and the pale-faced boy's world of wooden lodges.

"My almost-brother," Stands Straight whispered, "do not shout. Do not cry out."

Then the boy's face vanished from the crack. Stands Straight waited for the first cry of alarm, for musket barrels to appear. But all remained silent within the lodge.

7 IN SILENCE

Samuel

Samuel watched as Robert Nisbet looked around the cabin at the people gathered together on the rough benches. They had been sitting in silence for a long time. In his mid-thirties, Robert Nisbet was dressed exactly like the other men in the room, yet it seemed to Samuel that something set him apart. Samuel noticed the alertness of his eyes, as if he could look into the hearts of everyone there.

Father had talked often of this man. Robert Nisbet had been an indentured servant once. Now, wherever he went, he spoke against servitude and slavery. He had traveled widely, even among the French and the Indians. It was said that he could converse with the Indians.

Perhaps the Spirit will move him to give a message that will answer the questions troubling my heart, Samuel thought.

Robert Nisbet cleared his throat. Then he spoke in a voice as calm as his words. "The beloved of the Lord shall dwell in safety by Him. He shall cover thee with His feathers."

Zebulon Hoxsie, the clerk of the Meeting, nodded.

Samuel waited. But that was all. Again the silence grew.

Samuel looked toward his mother, who was sitting between Father and him. Sometimes Mother would speak when the Spirit moved her to do so. But she said nothing.

Samuel closed his eyes. His memory summoned words that Father had read aloud recently. He could remember them as clearly as he could picture the title, *Some Fruits of Solitude,* embossed in gold letters on the brown leather binding: "It were happy if we studied nature more and natural things, and acted according to nature whose rules are few, plain and most reasonable."

What is my nature? Samuel thought, shifting his weight on the bench. I feel like a dog whose back is up, ready to snap or growl at any moment.

"Samuel, look for the Light Within," was what Father would say.

Samuel let out a small sigh. As he did so, a tingle went down his spine. It was the same feeling he'd had earlier in the day, the feeling of being watched. He turned his head and looked toward the rough log wall by his right shoulder. Through the chink between the logs he could see the edges of forest close to the cabin, even a bit of the rolling hills to the east. There was a stone wall at the edge of Zebulon Hoxsie's fields, much like the one that he had worked so hard to build. Samuel stared at the wall and at the woods. He studied every rock and bush and tree. But he saw nothing else, not even a bird.

That is strange, he thought. There were always birds in the trees at this time of day. But today there were none. It was as if all the land around them was also sitting in silence, waiting for something.

Mother put her hand on his. He turned back toward her and looked up. He saw concern on her face.

She knows, Samuel thought. She knows I am ready to fight if I have to. I will fight the English or the Indians or anyone who tries to harm my family. I will use sticks and stones if I have to, but I will fight. Then no one can call me a coward.

Samuel leaned his shoulder against the wall and

tried to listen for the Voice inside himself. It was so hard to do. He was not like Mother or Father or Jonathan. They sat patiently, waiting for words to come from within. It was so quiet that Samuel could hear the creaking of the wood in the benches and the sound of people breathing.

At some Meetings there might be one person who would feel led to talk at length. Samuel remembered the Meeting they had gone to when he was very young, back when they lived in Provincetown. He had learned then to look toward Father when someone was speaking. Father's face, carefully turned toward the speaker, would always show that he was listening.

Father was not one who talked much, so his words had weight. Samuel remembered what Father had said to him about silence and listening.

"God hath made us with two ears and but one mouth, Samuel. So we must spend double the time in listening that we spend in speech."

Perhaps Father would be led to speak now. But his father said nothing, and Samuel's own uneasiness grew.

Samuel leaned against the log wall and looked out again through the logs. Then a shock went down his back like a handful of snow. He breathed in hard and bit his lip.

He had seen a man standing there, looking straight at the Meetinghouse. The man had quickly disappeared, but Samuel had seen how his brown face was painted. He was an Indian!

Samuel pulled back from the wall and reached over to grasp Father's sleeve. Father turned to look at him, surprise on his face.

Samuel pointed toward the crack in the wall. He mouthed the word without speaking it out loud. Even though he knew that Father understood him, he kept on saying it silently: *Indians. Indians. Indians.* He repeated it over again, until Mother gently placed her finger on Samuel's lips.

The air in the cabin felt thick. Samuel reached down to grasp the new walking stick he had placed on the floor. He clenched his right hand so tightly around the stick that it seemed as if the wood would splinter. If he were alone and the Indians were to appear, he would not have to think. He would raise up his stick to smite the Indians like Samson.

But what would the Indians do to the others at Meeting if he fought? It might make them angrier. The rumors he had heard about the Indians made him afraid. They hated white people. They were bloodthirsty. In his mind Samuel saw his family's hen yard the morning after a weasel had slipped in: the chickens dead, blood spattered everywhere. Worse than weasels—that was how other people spoke of the Indians. And those whom they did not kill would be taken captive and tortured.

Samuel tried to remember what his father had told him about Indians. The Light of God was in them too. He struggled to keep that in his mind, but it did not ease his fear.

Father reached over to grasp his right wrist. Father's face was calm, but his knuckles were as white as Samuel's as he held on to his son's arm.

Samuel continued to clutch the stick. Then he heard the creak of the Meetinghouse door as it opened wide.

8 MEETING

▼

Stands Straight | Samuel

Sees-the-Wind motioned in Stands Straight's
direction. The boy came out from behind the wall
and stood by his uncle. They were still far enough
from the wooden lodge that it would be hard for
anyone to hit them with a musket shot.

Sees-the-Wind lifted his right hand and made a
circle above his head. Then he lowered his hand
down by his shoulder and dropped it palm down
toward the earth. It was the signal for the others to
come to him. Together they would move slowly
toward the wooden lodge.

Stands Straight watched as his uncle began to
walk across the open ground between the shelter
of the stone wall and the wooden lodge. It was an
act of either great courage or foolishness to walk
in such a way toward a place where enemies might

be waiting. Yet Stands Straight felt a weight lift from his heart as his uncle began that walk. He followed close behind, and because the other men also trusted the judgment of Sees-the-Wind, they did the same.

Stands Straight saw how his uncle held his bow loosely at his side. The arrow that his index finger held against the bow was no longer nocked on the bowstring, ready to be fired. Stands Straight knew that this did not mean his uncle was unready. A bow in his uncle's hands was more dangerous than a musket, which could only be fired once and then would take many heartbeats to reload. He had watched Sees-the-Wind pick up a bow and a quiver of arrows and—in less time than it took to clap one's hands four times—fire four arrows into a target.

Now Stands Straight was close enough to the door to see that it had no lock. His uncle pushed open the door, ducked his head under the doorway, and stepped through, with Stands Straight behind him.

As Sees-the-Wind stood there, looking around the small room, none of the white people spoke. No one shouted. No one moved from the place where he sat.

"Unh-hunh," Sees-the-Wind said in a very soft voice.

Sees-the-Wind took another step further into the room, closer to the people on the benches. One man lifted his head and gazed into the eyes of Sees-the-Wind. Stands Straight saw that this man was the father of his almost-brother. He liked this man who looked at them as if he were looking up at friends.

Stands Straight looked next at his almost-brother, who sat by the wall. The mother sat there too, and also the little brother. The young man, whose shoulders were very broad and whose face was very red, held his walking stick in his hand. Stands Straight saw, as he knew his uncle had seen, that the stick was the only object in that whole room which might be used as a weapon. Stands Straight gazed at his almost-brother, and his almost-brother looked back at him.

The Indian who stood there, filling the doorway, was the tallest man Samuel had ever seen. The two heron feathers that rose from the cap on his head brushed the roof of the Meetinghouse. Samuel could see that the Indian was at least a head taller than his own father, who was not a small man. Yet that big man had slipped in through the door of the cabin as quietly as a breath of wind crossing the meadow. The big Indian held a bow and arrow

in his hand. He stood there calmly, looking around the Meeting, peering intently into one face after another.

Someone moved behind the tall man. It was an Indian boy. He too was tall, and held himself very straight—though his head only came up to the older man's shoulder. And while that tall man looked into the face of Samuel's father, the slender young Indian did something very strange. He lifted up a stone that he held in his right hand, shut one eye, and then squinted through the hole in the stone as if it were a spyglass. He surveyed the room and then looked through the hole directly at Samuel.

Samuel felt afraid at first. But as the tall boy continued to look steadily at him—as if trying to understand him—Samuel felt the fear leave his own heart. Then Father—as if he, too, felt that tension leaving his son—released his grip. Samuel opened his hand and placed his walking stick on the floor.

Stands Straight was surprised. Never before had he seen so many white people sit so long without speaking. He had heard it said that the whites were born talking and never stopped until they died. They spoke so much that they often forgot how to hear. But these white people were not talkers. They were listeners. And looking through his eye stone he saw what they were listening to. They were listening to hear the voice of *Ktsi Nwaskw*, the Creator, that voice which is hidden in each person's heart. They looked as if they would sit as long as it would take the sun to move the width of two hands across the sky.

"*Nidoba*," someone said. "My friend." It was a brown-haired Bostoniak man who looked to be of middle years and not of a great height.

"*Nidoba*," Sees-the-Wind replied, speaking softly.

The brown-haired man stood, a smile on his face. He walked over to Sees-the-Wind and held out his hand. Sees-the-Wind took the hand of friendship that was offered to him and shook it.

"*Kwai, nidoba*," said the brown-haired man, speaking in Abenaki. Then he continued in French. "My name is Nisbet. You are welcome here."

"Nizbed, are there weapons here?" Sees-the-Wind asked in French.

"*Non*," the brown-haired man called Nizbed answered. "All here are the people of peace." He motioned with his right hand toward an empty bench. "Join us."

Sees-the-Wind turned and leaned out the door

to carefully place his bow and his arrows against the outside wall of the Meetinghouse. Then he went to sit on the bench. One after another, all the Abenakis did the same with their weapons and took empty seats among the Bostoniak men and women. The last to enter and sit down, looking as nervous as two deer walking into the lair of a panther, were Richard and Hungry Frenchman.

They all sat in silence.

9 PARTING

▼

Samuel

As they sat together, Indian and Friend alike, Samuel kept looking over at the Indian boy who had come to sit beside him. Although he was no longer afraid, Samuel was still not sure how he felt. So much had happened so quickly.

Finally the sense of stillness changed. Zebulon Hoxsie extended the hand of friendship to the tall Indian man next to him. The Indian man took the clerk's hand without hesitation. In the manner of Friends at the breaking of Meeting, everyone was shaking hands with neighbors on either side, in front or in back.

It was natural for Samuel to reach out to the young Indian boy sitting next to him. The boy shifted the stone he held to his left hand, and with his right hand he shook Samuel's.

Indians and Friends were standing and greeting one another. The handshake of peace was passed around the room.

Robert Nisbet, Zebulon Hoxsie, and the tall Indian man with the heron feathers on his head led them all to Friend Hoxsie's house, a mile and a half away. People were talking. Samuel heard words that he knew must be French and other words which he did not know. Indian words. The young Indian boy, who kept lifting that stone to his face to look through it, stayed close to Samuel as they walked, matching his steps to Samuel's limping pace. Jonathan hurried to catch up to them.

"*Nidoba,*" the young Indian said, placing his hand first on Jonathan's shoulder and then on Samuel's. Jonathan beamed, but Samuel did not know what to say.

When they arrived at Zebulon Hoxsie's house, bread and cheese were placed on a table. Samuel picked up one of the wooden trays with cheese on it and thrust it toward the Indian boy.

"Here," Samuel said. "Eat."

The Indian boy reached out his hand and delicately picked up a piece of cheese. Samuel noticed how long and slender the boy's fingers were.

"*Wliwini,*" said the Indian boy. Then, seeing

that Samuel did not understand, he spoke his thanks again in French. *"Merci."*

Samuel smiled.

The boy smiled back at him. He placed his hand on Samuel's left shoulder and then on his own. Then he spoke further words in Abenaki. He looked over at Robert Nisbet, who was now standing near them.

"He is telling thee that his name is Stands Straight," Robert Nisbet said. "And that he will always be thy friend, *nidoba,* as thou art his."

When they finished eating, Sees-the-Wind spoke to Robert Nisbet, who asked his host for a hammer and two nails. Then all of them followed Sees-the-Wind back to the front of the Meetinghouse. Robert Nisbet took the hammer and drove the nails, side by side, into the wood above the Meetinghouse door. The tall Abenaki man held up one hand and began to speak in French.

"He says to us," Robert Nisbet translated, "that his name is Sees-the-Wind. He and the others came here because they were asked by the English to make war on the Americans. Before they fought, they wanted to see what kind of people we were. They surrounded our house, thinking they might destroy all who were within. But when they saw us sitting with our door open and without weapons of defense, they had no disposition to hurt us. Then they knew that they would not take the side of the king. They would take the side of peace. They will return to their own people. They will not fight in this war between King George and his children."

Sees-the-Wind held up an arrow in both hands. He broke off the arrowhead and dropped it into the pouch at his side. Then he placed the arrow over the door to the Meetinghouse, balancing it on the two nails.

"This arrow," said Sees-the-Wind as Robert Nisbet translated his words into English, "is our mark. It will not protect you from your own people. But those of my people, the Abenaki, who see this will do you no harm. They will know you are the people of peace."

Samuel looked at Stands Straight. The Abenaki boy was holding the eye stone up toward Samuel's face. Samuel leaned forward and felt the coolness of the stone against his cheek as he looked through it. Stands Straight placed one hand on Samuel's shoulder and then moved the stone, directing Samuel's gaze toward the Meetinghouse, the people gathered near it, his parents, and then the wide valley and the mountains beyond.

Samuel saw the creases that formed at the edge of his father's eyes as he smiled at the hungry-looking Frenchman still stuffing bread and cheese into his mouth. He saw the carefully piled stones of the walls that marked the Friends' everyday work and their caring for this land. He saw the wind rippling the heron feathers on the cap of the tall Indian who had said he would take the side of peace. And he knew he was not a coward. He knew this as if he were looking through his own heart.

Stands Straight removed the stone. Then he tapped it against his chest before placing it in the pouch by his side. He looked at Samuel to see if he understood. Slowly Samuel reached up one hand to touch his eye and then his own chest.

Stands Straight placed his right hand on his heart and then held his hand out toward Samuel. Samuel reached out his own right hand and took the hand of the tall Indian boy.

"*Nidoba*," said Stands Straight.

"Friend, *nidoba*," Samuel answered.

Sees-the-Wind turned, faced north, and walked across the field. Without looking back, Stands Straight and the others in his party followed.

Samuel made a circle with the thumb and fore-finger of his right hand and looked at the arrow over the door. Then he turned and, through that same circle of the heart's vision, watched until the Indians disappeared from sight.

Author's Note

I was a child growing up near Saratoga Springs, New York, when I first heard the story that is the historical basis for *The Arrow Over the Door*. I believe it was a Methodist minister, Paul Hydon, who told me the tale of a group of hostile Indians coming to the Friends (Quaker) Meetinghouse in nearby Easton, New York, during the Revolutionary War, seeing that the people gathered there were people of peace, and being so moved that they embraced them as friends. That story from what in 1777 was called "Saratoga Meeting," and is now known as "Easton Meeting," stuck with me over the years. It came back to mind when I read a version of it sometime in the 1980's in a local newspaper.

But it was not until the 1990's that I began to seriously

think about its possibilities as a historical novel for young readers. I stood in Easton on the site of the events that took place more than two centuries ago and a voice within me spoke, saying, "Tell this story. Tell it now." I made a proposal to my editor at Dial, Cindy Kane, and her enthusiasm for the idea was matched only by the feedback and intelligent suggestions she gave me along every step of what was to prove to be a long and sometimes twisting trail.

The research that I did went in two directions—Indian and Quaker. The Friends of eighteenth-century America are a people almost as little known to modern Americans as their Native American contemporaries. The following description was kindly provided by the members of the Easton Monthly Meeting:

Although Friends' worship is rooted in the Bible, early Friends were distinguished from their European Christian contemporaries in belief as well as practice. Quakers have no creed or codified statement of faith. Rather, they use a book of Faith and Practice, collected experiences and revelations of individual Friends which grew out of the spiritual seeking of George Fox.

Born in 1624, George Fox became a charismatic preacher and visionary in the midst of a great religious awakening in seventeenth-century England. People were opposing the clergy's control of their faith and practice. Fox and his followers proclaimed the Inner Light of God to be in every person.

Out of the search to keep their faith continually vital and to follow the leadings of the Inner Light, Friends developed many of the "peculiar" practices of their worship and living, characterized by an emphasis on simplicity and equality. Meetinghouses are traditionally simple buildings, with no altars, crosses, icons, or ornamentation. Clothing and speech were simple as well, with "thee" and "thou" being used for all persons, omitting the "you" form used in those days for superiors. There was even a testimony against using the "pagan" names for days and months, so they used numbers for both instead of the common names we know today. There was no swearing of oaths of loyalty or allegiance, and no observation of traditional Christian holidays, as Friends believed that every day was the Lord's.

At the heart of Friends' practices is the silent Meeting for Worship, with no clergy, no music, no sacraments, no ceremonies to interfere with each individual's direct relationship with God. Friends gather to "meet" God, waiting together in the silence for "leadings of the Spirit" to guide their words and actions. In the 1770's, testimonies arising from the leadings of the Spirit would have included opposition to war, abolition of slavery, and equality of the sexes. Friends in the late twentieth century still hold with their earlier founders that the power of God's love alone should cause us to "quake" in our boots. Hence, members of the Religious Society of Friends are still referred to as Quakers.

Though the Russells are fictitious characters, their actions and attitudes are meant to reflect those of a Quaker family of that time. I came away from my research with a new respect for the courage and integrity of Friends. They held fast to their beliefs when threatened with imprisonment or death in both England and America (where the Puritans suppressed overt Quaker practice). Among the many European religious traditions brought to America, the Friends have a strong record in their dealings with American Indians. Both before and long after the 1777 incident, the Friends were praised by Indians for their honesty and spirit of true brotherhood. When Ely S. Parker, a Seneca Indian, became the first Native American Commissioner of Indian Affairs under President Grant, he replaced corrupt Indian agents with Quakers.

The more I read, the more I realized how important the Easton Meeting story was to Friends. One version of it, a story from *A Book of Quaker Saints* (1917) by the British author L. Violet Hodgkin, is called "Fierce Feathers." It seemed to be known in many Friends Meetings—not only in the United States, but throughout the world, for it has been translated into other languages.

As I researched, however, I began to find inconsistencies between Hodgkin's story and historical fact. It was at that point that I called on my younger sister, Marge Bruchac, for help. One of Marge's special areas of expertise is the histories and traditions of both Native and non-Native people in the colonial period. She is a Consulting Interpreter for Native American Cultures for Old Sturbridge Village and other New England museums. Many long phone conversations and much documentation later, we emerged with a story that was substantially different from the one I thought I might be telling. (It also turned out to be a story that was connected in unexpected ways to my own family.)

Marge was so generous with her help, which was so crucial to the historical accuracy of this book, that I consider her as much a coauthor as a source of information. Several important changes in direction came as a result of her assistance. She and I also were greatly helped by the numerous

Friends—too many to cite individually, but I thank them all—who provided us with resource materials and advice. In particular, I thank the members of the Easton Monthly Meeting, who read and discussed the manuscript and made valuable suggestions. Their version of the Quaker-Indian encounter, which they call "Feathers of Peace," reflects the spiritual awareness of both their Quaker ancestors and the Indians who came to the Meetinghouse that day. The people of Easton Meeting continue to find inspiration from this event. Each year in early September the telling of the story is a part of Easton Day, which is devoted to bringing the spirit of yesterday's story into their lives today.

When I first outlined the story, I thought that it would take place in 1775, just before the Revolution. That was the date in Hodgkin's popular version. But research into the earliest written Quaker records shows that the date of the actual Indian-Quaker encounter was two years later—1777. Further, it took place just before the battles of Saratoga, which were pivotal events in American history. A fine essay entitled "Feathers of Peace" (*Quaker History,* Volume 65, Spring 1976) by Dorothy M. Williams, former clerk of the Easton Friends Meeting, was very helpful in clearing up historical details and introducing me to the earliest accounts.

I also first assumed that the Indians in the story were Mohawk. It seemed logical, since the Mohawk leader Joseph Brant (Thayandanega) and his Mohawk volunteers were the primary Indian allies of the British at the time. But, as Marge and I did our research, we found evidence of many different Indian nations present in the area—some neutral, some allied with the British, and some on the American side. One little-known fact, for example, is that the Stockbridge Mohicans or

Muhheakunnuk, then living in a mission village near an ancient homesite in the Berkshires, formed an Indian militia in 1774 to help the American rebels. Nipmuck Indians from central Massachusetts fought in regiments alongside their Anglo-American neighbors at Saratoga. Mahican, Wappinger, Mohegan, Schaghticoke, Pequot, and Mohawk Indians were present at the Saratoga battles in 1777, and even people from the Ottawa and Wyandot nations farther west.

According to the earliest accounts, there were two Frenchmen with the party of Indians who appeared at that Friends Meeting, and one Friend conversed with the leader of the group in French. At that time there were many French and even English who lived among and dressed like their Indian friends—just as there were a great many Indians living among and dressing like European-Americans. (On the American frontier of the eighteenth century the line between white and Indian was often blurred with regard to dress, language, and housing.) But if the Indians did speak French, where would they have come from at that time? The most logical answer was from Canada to the north. I felt a strange sensation of connection. Although there were French-speaking Mohawks, it was more likely that Indians traveling through would be Abenaki—my own Native heritage. Not only were the Abenakis fluent in French, they were being courted by both rebel American and loyal British troops as scouts and allies.

After the death of Jane McCrea, the fiancée of a British officer, who was killed—possibly by accident—by Indians in July 1777 near Fort Edward, New York, the British sternly reprimanded the Indians they held responsible. Those Indians—particularly the Huron, the Ottawas, and Wyandots—were insulted by the reprimand and deserted General

Burgoyne's army in great numbers. To fill in the ranks, the British were actively recruiting Indians who had been the former allies of the French, such as the Abenaki. With this sequence of events in mind, I decided to make the Indians in this story a newly arrived party of Abenakis who had doubts (as did many of the Indians on both sides) about their part in this white man's war. I also discovered that the American officer who was most influential in convincing the Abenakis to either remain neutral or join the American side was a man named Timothy Bedel. My wife, Carol, is a direct descendant of Bedel.

The earliest and most extensive account of the Easton Meeting Indian story was in a report by a committee of Friends to the Meeting for Sufferings of New York Yearly Meeting. Dated "1st mo. 9th, 1787," it reads:

A party of Indians with two Frenchmen surrounded the [Meeting] house; one of the Indians after looking in, withdrew and beckoned with his hand upon which a Friend went out and was asked by signs whether there [were] soldiers there, the Indian shook hands with him and the rest came into the house; they were marked, painted and equipt for War, and it being about the conclusion of the Meeting, they shook hands with Friends, and one Friend having the French tongue could confer with them with the assistance of the two Frenchmen. When they understood Friends were at a Religious Meeting, they went to one of their houses got victuals of which a prisoner with them partook, and they departed.

Readers may notice that in my story I eliminated the prisoner said to be with the Indians in this report. Native attitudes toward prisoners were complex. They might be held for ransom or, as I have tried to suggest in the Abenaki characters' thoughts about capturing Samuel, taken as replacements for missing family members. Rather than raise such a complicated issue in a story of this length, I chose to omit the character altogether.

In 1833 an account verified by Zebulon Hoxsie (who was the first clerk of Easton Meeting) identifies the French-speaking Friend as Robert Nisbet, who "had felt a concern to walk through the then wilderness and sit with Friends at their weekday Meeting." The historical details about Nisbet in my story are accurate and he actually did, according to other accounts, make the comment at that Meeting about "covering thee with feathers." The 1833 account concludes with these words: "Zebulon Hoxsie, one of the Friends present then invited them to his house, put a cheese and what bread he had on the table and invited them to help themselves. They did so and went quietly and harmlessly away."

One detail, which appears to have been an invention of Hodgkin's, is the placing of a feather over the door of the Meetinghouse by the "fierce" leader of the Indians (who himself wears a multicolored band of feathers unlike anything this side of the Western plains!). This detail is repeated in other retellings of Hodgkin's story.

I have never heard of a feather being placed over a door as a sign of peace, but I have heard of the shape of an arrow being drawn on a wall or an actual arrow (without a point) being placed over a doorway as a sign of friendship. I believe that it is very likely that those Indians did do something to mark the Meetinghouse as a place of peace, a place under their protection. Thus I changed the feather to an arrow and put bows and arrows into the hands of the Indian characters.

Reflecting attitudes prevalent at the time that Hodgkin's story was published, over eighty years ago, the Indians in "Fierce Feathers" were portrayed as stereotypically savage and warlike. Described as having "evil" faces, "cruel" grins, clutching poisoned arrows "only too ready to fly, and kill," they symbolized what Hodgkin called "the power of hate." I believe it is quite possible that the Indians were looking for that Friends Meeting because they knew Robert Nisbet (who was well-known as a friend of the Indians) and had no warlike intentions at all. However, it is also possible that when they reached Easton Meeting, they did not know what was going on and were undecided about their course of action.

I've opted for the second possibility because of its dramatic possibilities and because it shows that a true commitment to peace can transcend race and culture. I hope the story may remind us all that the way of peace is a road which can be walked by all human beings.

Joseph Bruchac, who is of Abenaki Indian and European origin, is the author of numerous books for children and adults. Many are about American Indians, including *The Heart of a Chief* and the picture book *The First Strawberries*.

James Watling has created artwork for many books with historical themes, ranging from the first Thanksgiving to the Great Depression.